To goblins and ghouls
And all dogs that drool
To dressing and turkey
And pets that are quirky!

Printed in the United States of America
First Printing, 2020
ISBN: 978-1-7330943-4-4

A Silly Milly Fall

Written by Sheri Wall

Illustrated by Ilona Stuijt

Designed by Erin Riddle

My *Milly* is so very *silly*
She loves when the fall air gets *chilly*
She'll shake and she'll roll
As we take a long stroll
We jog down the path *willy-nilly!*

We head out for the day on a *road trip*
In the wind her big ears do a *backflip*
She prepares to explore
There are pumpkins galore
Milly signals her pick with a loud *yip!*

It's time that we find her a costume
We search in the closet and bedroom
Milly what do you think
Pretty princess in pink
Or zombie or witch with a straw broom?

Now *Milly* and I give our porch *flare*

Jack-o-lanterns with carved eyes that just *stare*

So many surprises

And spooky disguises

A mummy and ghoul in a green *chair!*

The house is all ready for greeting
New friends and our neighbors we're meeting
Milly sniffs all the sweets
As kids take to the streets
For a long night of fun trick-or-treating!

The doorbell is ringing and ringing
So Milly decides to start singing
She sits right on cue
And shakes some hands too
Watch out while that tail is swinging!

The stars and the moon shine their bright light

House quiet, a little past midnight

And then I remember

The month is November

For now I'll just let Milly sleep tight.

I work in the yard with my Milly
She runs through the leaves willy-nilly
I go grab a rake
Then sense a backache
Oh Milly, I'd rather be silly!

It's time that we prep the big meal

Roast turkey of course is ideal

Mashed potatoes and peas

Milly's eyes say yes please

But who can I get to help peel?

The table we'll set to look just so
Napkins and plates in a straight row
Milly gives me a smirk
To approve of the work
Tall candles will shimmer a soft glow.

The dinner was so *satisfying*
Now dishes need washing and *drying*
The gravy is sticking
But *Milly* is licking
I can tell that she really is *trying!*

We relax and turn on some *football*

Yet *Milly* escapes down the long *hall*

She returns through the door

To find out the score

And barks as the ref makes a bad *call*.

Full tummies are causing some snoozing

So Milly appears to be choosing

Who has the best lap

For a Dane's cozy nap

Oh Milly, you sure are amusing!

As fall slips away willy-nilly

There's so much to learn from sweet Milly

Be thankful, be true

Be kind and be you

And never forget to be silly!

Also available in Milly's silly collection:

Silly Milly the DANE

Illustrated b...

A Silly Milly Christmas

Illustrated by Ilona Stuijt Written by Sheri Wall Designed by Erin Riddle

A Silly Milly Birthday

Illustrated by Ilona Stuijt Written by Sheri Wall Designed by Erin Riddle

Sheri Wall is a wife, mom, Great Dane aunt, Texan, and an award-winning children's book author. She uses rhymes and repetitive verse as essential learning tools in her writings. Sheri enjoys cooking, eating, decorating, bargain hunting, and being active. See more of Sheri's books at amatterofrhyme.com.

Ilona Stuijt is a traveling artist and illustrator from the Netherlands. She has worked on more than twenty books for children and adults. Ilona's paintings and illustrations are spread all over the globe. See Ilona's unique style at lankyartist.com.

Erin Riddle is a vintage-style photographer at Lone Star Pin-up and Vintage Luxe in Texas. In addition to loving Great Danes, she also enjoys singing, shopping, and entertaining friends and family. She is excited to share a little silliness with everyone during her favorite time of year through her lovable stinkmuffin, Milly.

Made in United States
North Haven, CT
29 September 2021